D0687142

DON'T BUG ME!

LANDMARK EDITIONS, INC.

P.O. Box 270169 • 1402 Kansas Avenue • Kansas City, Missouri 64127

(816)241-4919

written and illustrated by

Gillian McHale

Dedicated to:
My mom and dad for all their love and creative inspiration. To Candace for sharing her writing talents and acting as my editor. And to Aliki for teaching me to think of myself as an author long before I was ever published.

International Standard Book Number: 0-933849-65-6 (LIB.BDG.)

Library of Congress Cataloging-in-Publication Data
McHale, Gillian, 1985-
Don't bug me! / written and illustrated by Gillian McHale.
p. cm.
Summary: When insects and other pests invade her tree house, nine-year-old Leanna elicits help from her computer to defend her territory against the creepy, crawly creatures.
ISBN 0-933849-65-6 (lib.bdg. : alk. paper)
1. Children's writings, American.
[1. Tree houses—Fiction. 2. Pests—Fiction.
3. Children's writings. 4. Children's art.]

I. Title.
PZ7.M17754Do 1997
[Fic]—dc21 97-18802
CIP
AC

Creative Coordinator: David Melton
Editorial Coordinator: Nancy R. Thatch
Production Assistant: Brian Hubbard

Printed in the United States of America

Landmark Editions, Inc.
P.O. Box 270169
1402 Kansas Avenue
Kansas City, Missouri 64127
(816) 241-4919

DON'T BUG ME!

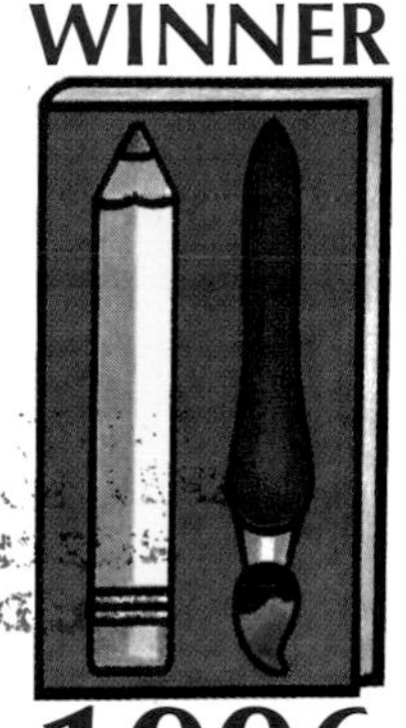

If anyone told Gillian McHale that she was outrageous, I am sure she would laugh heartily and say, "Thank you very much!" I don't think she has any interest in being considered as average or mediocre.

Gillian has a high-voltage brain, an abundance of raw energy, and a nonstop determination to succeed at whatever she attempts. She sets high standards for herself, and she regularly hits her targets. By eleven years of age, she has had not one, but two books published by commercial publishers. This could very well be a world's record.

In DON'T BUG ME!, Gillian has created the story of a girl who is not willing to sit by and allow insects to take over her tree house. The central character, Leanna Lane Willowbee, is quick-thinking, very verbal, quite determined, and often hilarious — not so different from the author herself.

DON'T BUG ME! was not an easy book to compose, for it is a network of bits and pieces, of actions and reactions, of factual information and imaginings. The text is sharp, quick, and to the point. Its humor is never jammed into the plot; it is allowed to come naturally from the situations that arise.

The illustrations are cleverly drawn and beautifully painted. They are skillfully developed to perfectly fit the personality of the book. Leanna Lane Willowbee looks and dresses exactly like her character should. That didn't happen by accident. It took careful thought and a countless number of sketches and designs.

Gillian has another very important quality. She understands that thorough editing and rewriting are necessary steps in refining a manuscript. She rewrote some of the sections in this book many times. I never once heard her complain. Instead, she would say, "Okay, let's try it again." I believe her rare insight and her willingness to "try it again" will serve her well throughout her life.

Thanks to Gillian McHale's perseverance, you are about to be transported to a beautiful summer morning, when Leanna Lane Willowbee eagerly rushes to her tree house and...well...

Hold onto your chairs — the fun is about to begin!

— David Melton
Creative Coordinator
Landmark Editions, Inc.

DURING THIS WARM SEASON, BIRDS MIGRATE NORTH TO BUILD NESTS AND RAISE NEW FAMILIES.
SUMMER IS A TIME OF NEW BEGINNINGS: SEEDS SPROUT AND YOUNG PLANTS GROW OUT OF THE EARTH.
AS THE WEATHER WARMS, HIBERNATING ANIMALS WAKE UP AND BEGIN TO SEARCH FOR FOOD.
TADPOLES AND SMALL AQUATIC ANIMALS RESPOND TO THE WARMTH AND WIGGLE TO LIFE IN PONDS AND STREAMS.
PASSWORD NEEDED FOR ENTRY

On the first morning of summer, it looked like it was going to be an absolutely perfect day! The sun shone brightly. There wasn't a cloud in the sky. Flowers filled the air with wonderful fragrances. Birds chirped happily as they gathered twigs for their nests. On the banks of the creek, frogs croaked lazily, and a turtle poked its head out of its shell to enjoy the warmth of the sun.

My name is Leanna Lane Willowbee. I am ten years old, and summer is my favorite time of year. I love swimming, roller skating, jumping rope, and playing baseball. But the best thing about summer is that I can spend lots of time in my tree house. I can do all sorts of things there. I can read. I can dream. I can imagine. Up in my tree house, I can travel anywhere I want to go and be anyone I wish to be.

That beautiful, sunny morning, I eagerly climbed the ladder to my tree house. I stepped onto the porch, walked through the doorway, and...I let out a bloodcurdling scream, *"AHHHHHHHHHHHHH!"*

I had stepped smack-dab in the middle of a huge spider web that was filled with ugly dead bugs! Dead bugs stuck to my nose. They stuck to my hair. They even stuck to my glasses. And lots of sticky cobwebs clung to my clothes and my face, making me itch all over!

I scrambled down the ladder and ran inside my house. In the bathroom I picked off all those disgusting bugs and brushed away the horrible cobwebs. I scrubbed my face and hands ten times...and then I scrubbed them again!

When I had finished, I grabbed a broom from the closet and stomped outside. I marched across the backyard and climbed the ladder to my tree house. As I charged through the doorway, I yelled:

"This is MY tree house! No bugs allowed!"

I swung the broom wildly! I chased that spider across the floor and swept it off the porch! I felt triumphant as I watched the invader fall to the ground below and skitter across the yard.

"And don't ever come back!" I shouted.

I stepped back inside and attacked the remaining cobwebs. I swept them from the rafters and brushed them from the corners of the room. I did not stop cleaning until I was absolutely sure that all the webs were gone.

For the rest of the day, I was Tarzan, living in my jungle tree house. High up in the treetops, I swung from vine to vine. When I gave out my mighty call, all the wild animals ran away in fear. No one dared to defy the great Tarzan of the Jungle or Leanna Lane Willowbee, the Mighty Spider Fighter of 1538 Greenbrook Way — except my mother, of course. When she called me to dinner, I knew I had better head for the house, and pronto!

Further adventures in my tree house would have to wait until tomorrow.

SOME SPIDERS HAVE BEEN KNOWN TO LIVE AS LONG AS TWENTY YEARS IN CAPTIVITY.

THE SILK OF A SPIDER'S WEB IS STRONGER THAN ANY MAN-MADE FIBER, EVEN STEEL CABLE

ONE TYPE OF SPIDER IS AS LARGE AS A DINNER PLATE.

A SPIDER'S WEB REFLECTS SUNLIGHT, WHICH ATTRACTS THE SPIDER'S PREY AND TRAPS IT.

MOST SPIDERS' VENOMS ARE NOT DANGEROUS TO PEOPLE.
SOME INSECTS AND SPIDERS USE CAMOUFLAGE THAT MAKES THEM LOOK LIKE LEAVES OR TWIGS.
SPIDERS IMMOBILIZE A PREY BY INJECTING VENOM INTO IT.
FEMALE BOMBARDIER BEETLES SHOOT A BOILING HOT PEPPER SPRAY INTO THEIR PREY.
SALE

The next morning I quickly ate my cereal. I was so eager for a new adventure in my tree house.

I hurried upstairs to my bedroom and opened the top drawer of my desk. My compass was there. I took it out and put it in my pocket.

My cat, Mr. Ferly, stretched and yawned as he watched me tie a red sash around my waist and get my plastic sword. After I put on a big hat and placed a black patch over my right eye, my outfit was complete. When I saw myself in the mirror, I was very pleased with the way I looked.

"All pirates beware!" I said boldly.

I pulled a wooden chest from under my bed and looked inside. My treasure map was still there, and so was my black and white flag. I smiled. I was sure that by nightfall, the chest would be filled with gold and precious jewels.

I closed the chest and carried it downstairs. As I started to step out the back door, my mother looked at me and said:

"Say hello to Long John Silver for me."

"I'll tell him *goodbye!*" I retorted. "The Seven Seas are no longer big enough for both of us."

When I climbed onto the porch of my tree house, Mr. Ferly, my trusty First Mate, was close behind. I pulled the chest up after me and opened it. I took out the flag and hoisted it to the top of the mast. Its menacing skull and crossbones flapped fiercely in the breeze. Standing at the ship's railing, I raised my sword high in the air.

"Ahoy, Mates! Prepare to sail!" I commanded.

With all the confidence of a fearless pirate captain, I strutted through the doorway of my cabin, and...I screamed, *"AHHHHHHHHHHHHH!"*

That spider had done it AGAIN! It had sneaked back and spun another web, and I was covered in the gooey stuff! I was furious! I stormed back to the house, frantically ripping off dead bugs and cobwebs as I went.

"Back so soon?" my mother asked.

"Don't bug me!" I grumbled as I headed toward the bathroom. I spent more than fifteen minutes picking, brushing, and washing. Then I hurried up to my bedroom.

My mother knew I was upset, and she followed me upstairs.

"What are you doing?" she asked.

"I am just checking out the enemy!" I answered determinedly.

"That sounds like a good idea," Mom said. Then she turned and walked away.

I knew my mother did not understand, but I didn't have time to explain things to her right then. I had a very serious situation on my hands. I plopped onto my chair and turned on my computer.

I selected the category: Encyclopedia

The computer instructed: *"Choose LISTING"*

I typed the word: BUGS

The computer responded: *"Try INSECTS"*

I typed: INSECTS

The computer told me: *"Select SPECIES"*

I typed: SPIDERS

The screen flashed red, then green, then yellow, and printed the message:

*"Spiders are **NOT** insects, Dummy!"*

"What a rude Mr. Know-It-All you are!" I scolded. "I certainly don't need a smart-aleck computer with a bad attitude problem! I just need you to tell me about spiders!"

"Spiders are not insects," the computer repeated, then quickly informed me, *"Spiders are arachnids because they have eight legs. Insects have only six legs. Now, Leanna Lane, is there anything else you want to know about spiders?"*

SPIDERS HAVE A 2-PART BODY WITH 8 JOINTED LEGS, BUT THEY DON'T HAVE WINGS.
INSECTS HAVE AN OUTSIDE SKELETON (EXOSKELETON), CONSISTING OF A 3-PART BODY WITH 6 JOINTED LEGS, AND MOST HAVE WINGS.
MANY PEOPLE ENJOY EATING THE POPULAR ARTHROPODS — CRABS AND LOBSTERS.
SPIDERS AND INSECTS ARE ARTHROPODS, BUT SPIDERS BELONG TO A DIFFERENT CLASS CALLED THE ARACHNIDS.
File Edit Encyclopedia
Insects
Spiders are NOT insects, Dummy!

PEOPLE CREATE PROBLEMS WHEN THEY MOVE INSECTS FROM THEIR NATURAL HABITATS.
ASIAN LONG-HORNED BEETLES CAME TO AMERICA ON SHIPS AND ARE NOW KILLING SUGAR MAPLE TREES.
WITHOUT NATURAL PREDATORS, INSECT NUMBERS WOULD BECOME UNCONTROLLABLE.
EURASIAN GYPSY MOTHS ARE THREATENING NORTH AMERICAN OAK TREES WITH EXTINCTION.

"Yes, I have another question. "How can I get a spider out of my tree house?"

"Are you bigger or smaller than the spider?"

"Bigger," I answered.

*"Then **big you** should pick up **little it** and throw **little it** out of the tree house!"*

"But, what if **little it** is full of **big poison**?"

"Not likely," explained the computer. *"Fewer than one percent of all spiders are poisonous to people."*

"Well, I don't want to take that chance," I said.

*"Then **big brave you** should chase **little spider** away with a **great big broom**."*

"I did that yesterday, but it came back."

"Well, now," the computer said. *"You **do** have a **stubborn little spider**. So **big brave you** will just have to capture **stubborn little spider**, take it far, far away, and leave it there."*

"No problem," I told the computer, and I flipped the switch to OFF.

I realized my mission could be dangerous. So I sneaked up the ladder to my tree house and peeked over the window sill. I took out my spyglass and scanned the room. I looked to the left. No sighting. I looked to the right. Nothing. I looked straight ahead. BINGO! There was the spider. It didn't even see me.

I quietly climbed through the window and tiptoed toward the spider. Then I made my move. I plunked a plastic jar over the spider and screwed the lid on tight. I carried the jar to the garage, jumped onto my bicycle, and sped away.

After I had ridden about four blocks, I came to an open field. I got off my bicycle, opened the jar, and shook the spider out. Wasting no time, I jumped back on my bicycle and headed for home.

"Mission accomplished!" I said proudly.

That afternoon Mr. Ferly and I set sail for a lost island in the Caribbean Sea. We filled our treasure chest with gold and precious jewels. Before leaving I had a fierce sword fight with Long John Silver. Then — I sank his ship!

I must say, it was a most pleasant afternoon! Mr. Ferly purred his agreement.

The next morning I cautiously made my way up to my tree house. But there was no need for concern. When I stepped inside, there was no spider, and no cobwebs were anywhere.

Mr. Ferly and I relaxed, but not for long. Fort Willowbee stood at the very edge of a wild frontier, and suddenly we were under attack. For most of the morning, Mr. Ferly and I fought off Genghis Khan and his Mongol tribesmen. We won, but the fight left us tired and very hungry.

So we sat down and ate the lunch I had packed. I ate a sandwich and drank a soda. Mr. Ferly gobbled down his favorite meal — sardines.

Before long I felt something tickle my leg. Then something tickled my hand. When I looked down, I saw that it wasn't just one some THING — it was a lot of some THINGS! My sandwich was being attacked by...ANTS!

"AHHHHHHHHHHHHH!" I screamed and dropped my sandwich. I jumped up, ran to the house, and got a can of bug spray.

As I stepped outside, my father saw me and asked, "What are you doing with that insecticide?"

"My tree house has been invaded by an army of ants! I'm going to spray every one of them!"

"Well," Dad said, "if you're going to do that, we had better get your mother, so the three of us can say *goodbye* to Mr. Ferly."

"Why should we tell Mr. Ferly *goodbye?"* I asked.

"Because you may be about to kill him," Dad replied.

"But you don't understand," I said. "I'm going to spray this stuff on the ants, not on Mr. Ferly."

"No, *you* are the one who doesn't understand," Dad told me. "If you spray the insecticide on the ants, they will get sick and die."

"That's my plan," I agreed.

"I know," Dad continued, "but when the birds eat the poisoned ants, the birds will get sick and die. And what does Mr. Ferly hunt in the backyard?"

"Birds," I answered quietly.

"Right," said Dad, "and if Mr. Ferly eats a bird that's full of insecticide, he could get sick and...well, it could be *Goodbye, Mr. Ferly!*"

"So why do you have bug spray?" I asked.

"I only use it in the house," he replied. "Not outside."

What should I do now? I wondered. But before I thought to ask my father how *he* would get rid of the ants, he had gotten into his car and driven away.

ANTS CAN LIFT FIFTY TIMES THEIR OWN WEIGHT. A HUMAN-SIZED ANT COULD LIFT A CAR.
TO FEED THEIR COLONIES, SOME ANTS PLANT GARDENS, HERD AND MILK APHIDS, AND ENSLAVE OTHER INSECTS.
ANTS CANNOT GET AS BIG AS HUMANS BECAUSE ANT LEGS COULD NOT SUPPORT THE WEIGHT.
ARMIES OF ANTS DEFEND THEIR COLONIES. ONE TYPE OF ANT WILL EVEN EXPLODE ITSELF TO DESTROY AN ENEMY.
POISON

I went up to my room, sat down in front of my computer, and turned it on.

"Back again?" the computer asked.

I didn't answer. I just typed the word: ANTS!

"Very interesting creatures," the computer responded. *"Ants are wonderful scavengers! They live in colonies and work together to clean up the garbage of the world."*

"I don't care about that," I said. "Some ants have invaded my tree house, and I want them to leave!"

"Do you have feet?" the computer asked.

"Of course I have feet — two of them!"

"Then use both of your feet to stomp on the invaders!" the computer ordered.

"I can't do that," I replied. "There are too many of them. Besides, that would make an awful mess on the floor."

"Then, let them eat cake!" the computer advised.

"Those ants are eating my sandwich, and you want me to give them a dessert, too!" I exclaimed.

The computer didn't respond. Instead, its screen went blank.

I left the room and returned to my tree house. For some time I watched in disgust as a long line of ants — now hundreds of them — marched in and out. They kept chewing away at my sandwich and carrying off crumbs.

"Let them eat cake. Let them eat cake," I kept muttering to myself.

Then, little by little, I began to understand what the computer meant. Finally, a super-duper idea formed in my mind.

I went to the kitchen and cut a large slice of chocolate cake. When I returned to my tree house, I started dropping cake crumbs across the floor to the edge of the porch, down the ladder, through the grass, under the fence, and into my neighbor's yard. The ants rushed to the crumbs and eagerly followed the path I had laid.

I felt like a modern-day *Pied Piper!* All by myself, I had gotten rid of those creepy crawly pests!

That afternoon Mr. Ferly and I floated off on a truly amazing journey in a hot-air balloon. We caused quite a stir when we landed in a town called Hamelin.

The villagers were having a terrible rat problem. I told them to bake a lot of chocolate cakes.

And that's how I became the hero of Hamelin.

OF THE 9,000 SPECIES OF ANTS, ARMY ANTS TAKE TOP HONORS FOR TEAMWORK.
ARMY ANTS MARCH ABOUT ONE FOOT PER MINUTE, CREATING A SOLID WALL OF ANTS UP TO 45 FEET ACROSS AND 3 TO 6 FEET LONG.
ARMY ANTS EAT SNAKES, LIZARDS, BABY BIRDS, AND OTHER THINGS THAT CANNOT RUN AWAY.
AT A STREAM, SOME ARMY ANTS LINK TOGETHER TO FORM A LIVING BRIDGE SO OTHERS CAN GO ACROSS SAFE AND DRY.
PASSWORD NEEDED FOR ENTRY

IN AFRICA, MOSQUITOES KILL MORE HUMANS AND OTHER ANIMALS THAN DO CROCODILES.
MOSQUITOES HAVE NO TROUBLE LOCATING HUMANS BECAUSE THEY SMELL THE CARBON DIOXIDE PEOPLE EXHALE.
MOSQUITOES USE THEIR NOSE (PROBOSCIS) LIKE A HYPODERMIC NEEDLE TO INJECT CHEMICALS.
GARLIC AND ALSO MOSQUITO REPELLENTS COVER THE SMELL OF CARBON DIOXIDE AND KEEP THE PESTS FROM FINDING US.
DRACULA
FERLY'S DAYOUT
THE FIRST DAY
DON'T BUG ME!!
WISHBONE

After dinner I went out to my tree house, carrying a blanket, a lantern, and a very scary book entitled *Beware of the Vampire!* To set the proper mood, I put a Dracula poster on the wall and wore a clove of garlic on a string around my neck.

As the full moon cast an eerie glow around me, I sat down and began reading:

> The townspeople dreaded the night of the full moon. For that was the time the bloodsucking monster emerged. The sound of fluttering wings made even the bravest tremble with fear.

I shivered a bit, pulled my blanket tighter around my shoulders, and continued reading:

> The vampire crept closer and closer to the beautiful lady. When he smiled, his sharp fangs appeared. Then he sank them deep into her neck, and...

"AHHHHHHHHHHHH!" I screamed.

I grabbed my neck and rushed to the house!

"Mom, a vampire bit me!" I cried.

My mother took a look. "Here's your vampire," she said as she laughed and held up a dead mosquito. Then she noticed swollen bites on my arms and legs. "Looks like you've been bitten by a lot of vampires," she mused.

"Well, don't scratch those bites," she warned as she rubbed lotion on me. They'll get infected."

I went to my room and turned on my computer.

I typed: Another Invader — MOSQUITOES!

"How many bit you?" the computer asked.

"More than 2,001!" I told him.

"Do not scratch those bites. They will get infected."

I already know THAT!" I replied. "I'm not stupid!"

"I will have to observe you longer before I can make a decision about the exact level of your intelligence."

"I don't need more of your insults," I bristled. "I just need to know how to get rid of mosquitoes."

"Mosquitoes are for the birds," the computer said.

"Is that statement meant to be a joke?" I asked.

"I am not programmed to tell jokes," replied the computer. Then the screen went blank.

"Your computer is correct," my father said from the doorway. "You need the help of some purple martins. Those birds love to eat mosquitoes."

The next day Dad and I purchased a martin house and set it on a high pole in the backyard.

We waited — two days, three days, a week. Finally four purple martins found the birdhouse. Soon they were zooming through the air, drawing mosquitoes into their mouths like vacuum cleaners. Dad and I watched with delight as the martins removed thousands of the little "vampires" from the sky!

A FLY'S COMPOUND EYES ALLOW IT TO SEE MOVEMENT FASTER THAN WE CAN.
FLIES CAN REACH SPEEDS OF 50 TO 70 MILES PER HOUR, SO THEY ARE DIFFICULT TO CATCH.
BECAUSE FLIES SEE MOVEMENT SO FAST, IT IS EASY FOR THEM TO GET AWAY.
THE BUZZING SOUND WE HEAR FLIES MAKE IS CAUSED BY THEIR WINGS BEATING AT A RATE OF 100 STROKES A MINUTE.

My dad's homemade ice cream is the best in the world! But that morning, there was only one scoop of it left. I put it in a dish and carried it to my tree house, licking my lips at the thought of enjoying every spoonful.

Spoon! I had forgotten to bring a spoon. I set the dish on the window sill and rushed back to the house. I returned to my ice cream, and...I screamed, *"AHHHHHHHHHHHHH!"*

"What's wrong?" I heard my mother call.

"My ice cream is covered with FLIES!" I yelled.

"Don't eat any of it!" she told me.

"But it's the last scoop!" I protested.

"That makes no difference," she replied. "It's not safe to eat!"

After I dumped the ice cream down the garbage disposal, I found myself in a familiar spot — in front of my computer. I turned it on and typed one word —

FLIES!

"Flies are very disgusting pests," the computer said.

"A whole squadron of them landed on my ice cream, and my mom wouldn't let me eat it!"

"Your mother is very wise. Flies are among the dirtiest pests in the world. They carry all kinds of germs. But that is not the most disgusting part." The computer paused for a moment, then asked, *"Do you want to hear the most disgusting part?"*

"Okay, tell me the most disgusting part."

"Well..." the computer explained. *"A fly cannot open its jaws. So it has a tubelike part on its face that hangs down with little needle points on the end of it. The fly spits saliva through the tube and onto the food. When the saliva hits the food, it turns the whole area into liquid. Then the hungry fly sips the liquid, like you sip milk shakes through a straw."*

"OH, GROSS!" I exclaimed. "How can I keep those filthy flies out of my tree house?"

"That's easy! Use SCREENS!" the computer replied smugly.

"I could have thought of THAT!" I snapped.

"Then why did you bother to ask me?" sneered the computer, and the screen went blank.

That afternoon Mom and I bought screens for my tree house. Together, we stapled them on the door and across the windows.

"Now my tree house is sure to be safe from all kinds of pests," I said happily.

It was time to celebrate my pest-free tree house. I called my friends, Heather and Mia. All I had to say were three magic words —

"SLUMBER PARTY TONIGHT!"

"I'll bring chocolate chip cookies," said Heather.

"I'll bring fudge brownies," offered Mia.

"I'll bring the rest," I told them.

I packed up corn chips, potato chips, and cheese puffs. Dad made his famous pizza for us. Mom filled a cooler with cans of soda. And we bought enough candy to feed sixteen hogs.

As soon as my friends and I entered my tree house, the fun began. We talked, we giggled, we munched, we crunched, we sipped sodas. Once it got dark, we told ghost stories.

Of course, I told my friends about the invading insects. They thought my battles with the creepy crawlies were hilarious.

"The ants came marching one by one, hurrah, hurrah!" sang Heather.

Mia laughed so hard tears streamed down her face. Then she howled, "Waiter, waiter, come quick! There's a fly on my ice cream!" Both of them roared with laughter then!

Their teasing was beginning to annoy me. But it became too much when Heather leaned forward, wiggled her fingers against my neck, and said, "Along came a spider and sat down beside her!"

"Don't bug me!" I yelled. I launched a chocolate chip frisbee in Heather's direction. She tried to catch it in her mouth. She missed, and the cookie hit the wall and crumbled on the floor next to a pile of potato chips and squashed cheese puffs.

Now I was really disgusted. "I'm going to bed," I told them. I spread out my sleeping bag and turned off the lantern.

Mia and Heather couldn't resist saying, "Ohhhh, Leanna — Sleep tight, and don't let the BED BUGS bite! Ha! Ha! Ha! Ha!"

It wasn't long before Heather and Mia had giggled themselves to sleep. I started to drift off, too, but lights outside suddenly began flashing on and off. When I crept to the porch, I saw hundreds of fireflies in the sky. With their flashing neon lights, they had spelled out the message —

SURRENDER OR ELSE!

I woke Heather and Mia. But by the time they looked out the window, the fireflies had gone. Of course, they said I had just imagined it. They laughed and laughed, and told me, "Fireflies can't spell!" Then they returned to their sleeping bags and giggled some more until they went to sleep.

But I had trouble getting to sleep. I kept wondering what the fireflies meant by "OR ELSE!"

INSECTS USE LIGHT AND SOUND TO SEND OUT MATING CALLS.
FIREFLIES USE THEIR LIGHTS TO SEND MESSAGES THAT ONLY OTHER FIREFLIES CAN UNDERSTAND.
SURRENDER OR ELSE!
INSECT SOUNDS CAN EXCEED 100 DECIBELS. THAT'S AS LOUD AS A JACKHAMMER.
SOME INSECT SOUNDS ARE SO ANNOYING THAT PEOPLE WILL LEAVE CERTAIN AREAS DURING THE SUMMER.

INSECTS ADAPT VERY QUICKLY BECAUSE MANY GENERATIONS OF INSECT YOUNG ARE BORN YEARLY.

ROACHES CAN INVADE ANYWHERE BY SLIDING THROUGH CRACKS AS THIN AS A PIECE OF PAPER.

COCKROACHES ARE DIFFICULT TO CATCH BECAUSE THEY CAN RUN FIVE FEET PER SECOND.

COCKROACHES ADAPT SO QUICKLY, THEY MIGHT BE THE ONLY SURVIVORS OF A NUCLEAR DISASTER.

I finally closed my eyes, but not for long. I was awakened by the pitter-pattering sounds of tiny feet that were scurrying across the floor. Then I heard the rattle of paper sacks and wrappers. I quietly reached for my flashlight, switched it on, and...I screamed, *"AHHHHHHHHHHHHHHHHHHHHHHHH!"*

Heather and Mia jumped up and screamed, too.

They're all over the place!" Mia screeched.

"Don't let them bite me!" Heather cried.

I should have paid more attention to the fireflies' warning! I should have known something terrible like this would happen!

"Let's get out of here!" I shouted.

The three of us scrambled down the ladder. As soon as we reached the safety of my bedroom, I typed a message to my computer —

HELP! COCKROACHES!! EVERYWHERE!!!

"Fascinating creatures," remarked the computer.

"They ruined our party!" I groaned.

"Then you should not have invited them."

"We didn't invite them!" I replied.

"Did you leave food on the floor?"

"Well...maybe a little bit," I admitted.

"That was the only invitation they needed," the computer explained. "*You see, cockroaches eat any kind of food that is left uncovered. They are among the world's best garbage disposals. Cockroaches are SUPER insects because they are SUPER survivors. They can live in most climates. They have been on Earth for millions of years, and they will be here a million years from now."*

"That's just fine and dandy," I said, "but as long as I'm on this Earth, I will not allow cockroaches in my tree house. Now, how do I get rid of them?"

"The answer is simple," the computer replied: *"Do not be such a slob! Pick up your own trash!"*

That did it! I was tired of being insulted by Mr. Know-It-All! I didn't bother to flip the switch to OFF. I just reached down and yanked the computer's plug from the wall socket!

For the rest of the night, my friends and I slept safely indoors in my bedroom.

Every story has a turning point. The night of the cockroaches was mine.

After Heather and Mia left the next morning, I did what I had to do. I picked up all the trash in my tree house, swept and mopped the floor, and washed the walls. I didn't leave even one tiny "invitation" for the cockroaches...the ants...the flies...or any of the other creepy crawlies. With screens on the door and the windows and no crumbs on the floor, my tree house was as bug-proof as I could make it!

During that summer, I learned a lot about insects and spiders. I learned that spiders spin very clever traps and help reduce the insect population. But I definitely do not want to have a spider for a house-guest or a roommate!

I realize that ants are great scavengers and work together in groups to clean up the earth. But I do not intend to invite them to any of my picnics!

Mosquitoes are a vital part of the food chain, and purple martins think these little pests are tastier than a banana split. But I refuse to be a personal blood bank for a swarm of thirsty vampires!

As for the flies and cockroaches — they provide a marvelous garbage disposal service for the world. But I do not want them spitting and nibbling on my food or crawling into things that belong to me...Oh, by the way, just wait until I tell you the latest...

My computer, Mr. Know-It-All, kept getting ruder every day and started acting even stranger and stranger. So Mom and I took it to the repair shop. Guess what the repairman found? *BUGS!* That's right. *BUGS!* Some little roaches had crawled inside and shorted out several circuits. The repairman said that this happens to computers all the time.

As soon as my computer was DE-BUGGED, its attitude improved immediately. No more "Mr. Know-It-All!" Now when I ask questions, the computer answers accurately, factually, and *very politely!*

Bugs! Bugs! Bugs! Like them or not, we need them. Without them, we would be up to our eyeballs in garbage in less than a month. So I have made an agreement with the creepy crawlies of the world. I have promised that I won't bug them if they won't bug me. And it is all working out very well, except... Wait a minute! I think there is something crawling up my arm...

"AHHHHHHHHHHHHHHHH!"

ENTOMOLOGISTS STUDY INSECTS TO HELP US MANAGE THEM AS A RESOURCE.
YOU CAN BE AN ENTOMOLOGIST AND TEACH OTHERS ABOUT THE AMAZING WORLD OF INSECTS.
WE HAVE ONLY BEGUN TO UNDERSTAND THE MANY BENEFITS INSECTS PROVIDE.
FOR INFORMATION: WRITE TO Y.E.S. (YOUNG ENTOMOLOGISTS SOCIETY), 1915 PEGGY PLACE, LANSING, MICHIGAN 48910.

BOOKS FOR STUDENTS BY STUDENTS!

Dav Pilkey age 19
Lauren Peters age 7
Benjamin Kendall age 7
Amy Hagstrom age 9
Michael Cain age 11
Leslie A. MacKeen age 9
Shintaro Maeda age 8
A. Chandrasekhar age 9
Dennis Vollmer age 6
Alise Leggat age 8

by Karen Kerber, age 12
St. Louis, Missouri
ISBN 0-933849-29-X Full Color

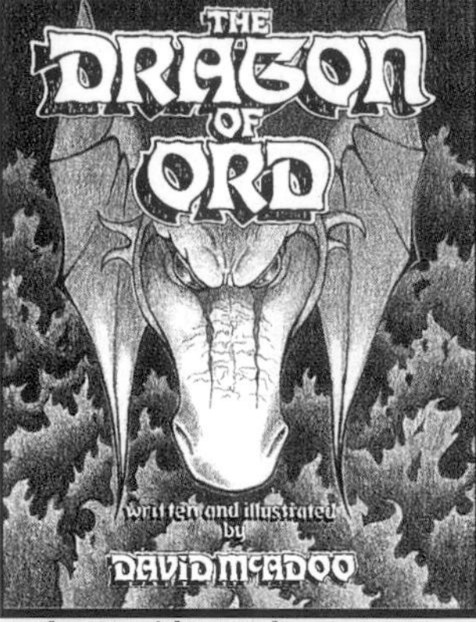

by David McAdoo, age 14
Springfield, Missouri
ISBN 0-933849-23-0 Inside Duotone

by Amy Hagstrom, age 9
Portola, California
ISBN 0-933849-15-X Full Color

by Isaac Whitlatch, age 11
Casper, Wyoming
ISBN 0-933849-16-8 Full Color

by Leslie Ann MacKeen, age 9
Winston-Salem, North Carolina
ISBN 0-933849-19-2 Full Color

by Elizabeth Haidle, age 13
Beaverton, Oregon
ISBN 0-933849-20-6 Full Color

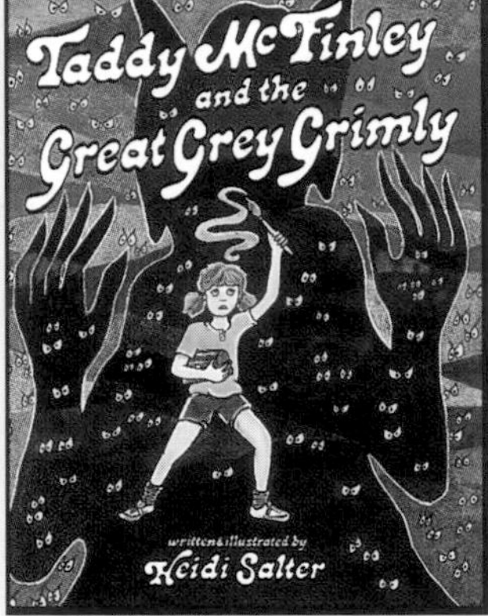

by Heidi Salter, age 19
Berkeley, California
ISBN 0-933849-21-4 Full Color

by Lauren Peters, age 7
Kansas City, Missouri
ISBN 0-933849-25-7 Full Color

by Aruna Chandrasekhar, age 9
Houston, Texas
ISBN 0-933849-33-8 Full Color

by Anika Thomas, age 13
Pittsburgh, Pennsylvania
ISBN 0-933849-34-6 Inside Two Colors

by Cara Reichel, age 15
Rome, Georgia
ISBN 0-933849-35-4 Inside Two Colors

by Jonathan Kahn, age 9
Richmond Heights, Ohio
ISBN 0-933849-36-2 Full Color

by Benjamin Kendall, age 7
State College, Pennsylvania
ISBN 0-933849-42-7 Full Color

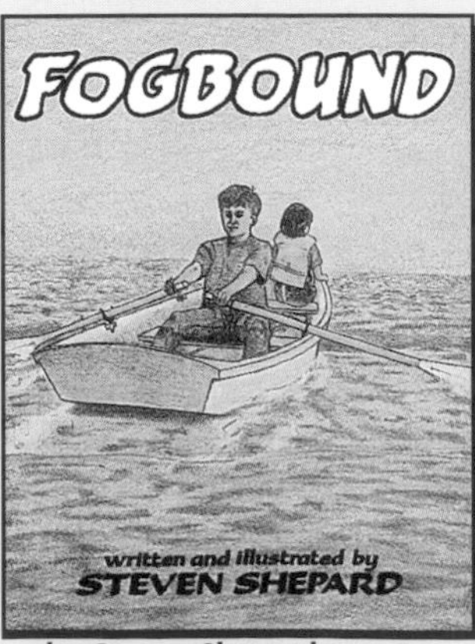

by Steven Shepard, age 13
Great Falls, Virginia
ISBN 0-933849-43-5 Full Color

by Travis Williams, age 16
Sardis, B.C., Canada
ISBN 0-933849-44-3 Inside Two Colors

by Dubravka Kolanović, age 1
Savannah, Georgia
ISBN 0-933849-45-1 Full Color

THE NATIONAL WRITTEN & ILLUSTRATED BY...AWARD WINNERS

by Dav Pilkey, age 19
Cleveland, Ohio
ISBN 0-933849-22-2 Full Color

by Dennis Vollmer, age 6
Grove, Oklahoma
ISBN 0-933849-12-5 Full Color

by Lisa Gross, age 12
Santa Fe, New Mexico
ISBN 0-933849-13-3 Full Color

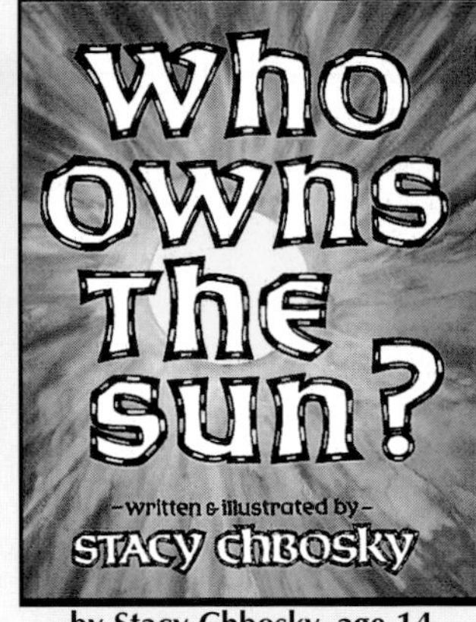

by Stacy Chbosky, age 14
Pittsburgh, Pennsylvania
ISBN 0-933849-14-1 Full Color

by Michael Cain, age 11
Annapolis, Maryland
ISBN 0-933849-26-5 Full Color

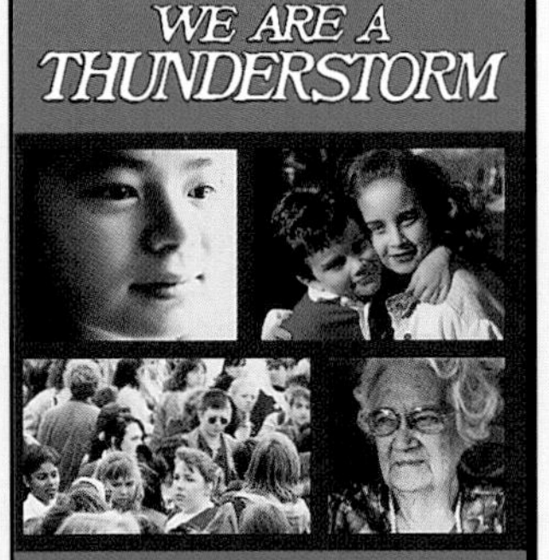

by Amity Gaige, age 16
Reading, Pennsylvania
ISBN 0-933849-27-3 Full Color

by Adam Moore, age 9
Broken Arrow, Oklahoma
ISBN 0-933849-24-9 Inside Duotone

by Michael Aushenker, age 19
Ithaca, New York
ISBN 0-933849-28-1 Full Color

by Jayna Miller, age 19
Zanesville, Ohio
ISBN 0-933849-37-0 Full Color

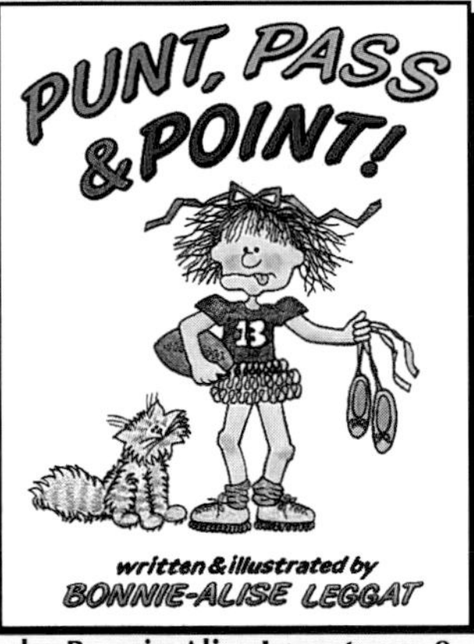

by Bonnie-Alise Leggat, age 8
Culpepper, Virginia
ISBN 0-933849-39-7 Full Color

by Lisa Kirsten Butenhoff, age 13
Woodbury, Minnesota
ISBN 0-933849-40-0 Full Color

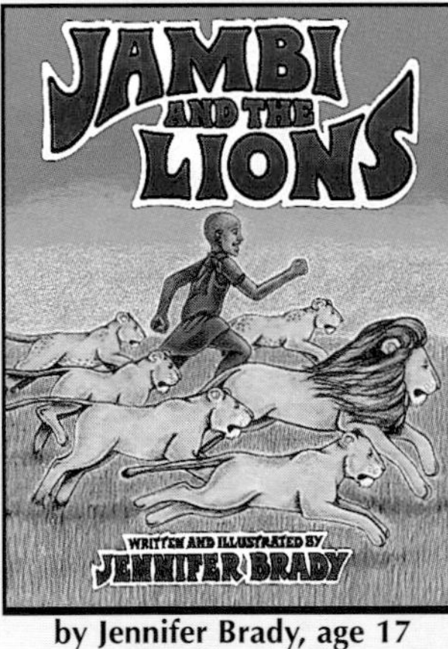

by Jennifer Brady, age 17
Columbia, Missouri
ISBN 0-933849-41-9 Full Color

by Amy Jones, age 17
Shirley, Arkansas
ISBN 0-933849-46-X Full Color

by Shintaro Maeda, age 8
Wichita, Kansas
ISBN 0-933849-51-6 Full Color

by Miles MacGregor, age 12
Phoenix, Arizona
ISBN 0-933849-52-4 Full Color

by Kristin Pedersen, age 18
Etobicoke, Ont., Canada
ISBN 0-933849-53-2 Full Color

Travis Williams
age 16

Anika D. Thomas
age 13

Isaac Whitlatch
age 11

Elizabeth Haidle
age 13

Miles MacGregor
age 12

Jayna Miller
age 19

Jonathan Kahn
age 9

Stacy Chbosky
age 14

David McAdoo
age 12

Amity Gaige
age 16

BOOKS FOR STUDENTS BY STUDENTS!

Bright Eyes and the Buffalo Hunt
Written and Illustrated by Laura Hughes

by Laura Hughes, age 8
Woonsocket, Rhode Island
ISBN 0-933849-57-5 Full Color

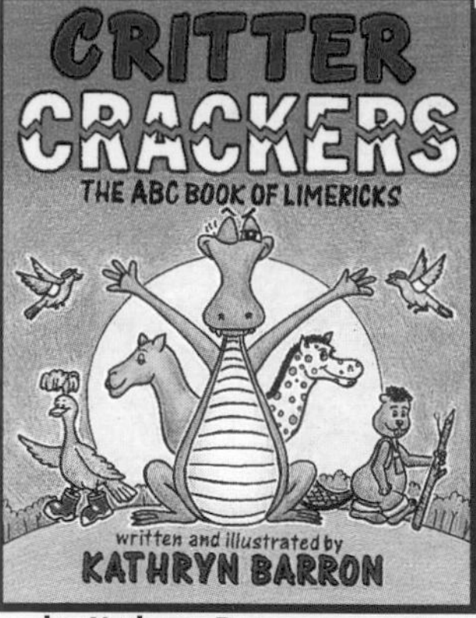

by Kathryn Barron, age 13
Emo, Ont., Canada
ISBN 0-933849-58-3 Full Color

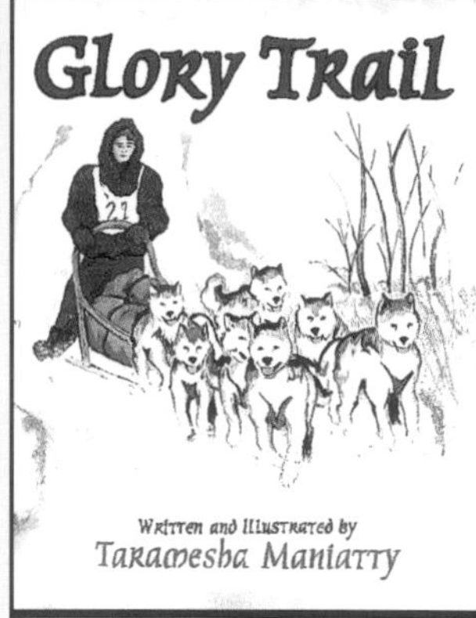

by Taramesha Maniatty, age 15
Morrisville, Vermont
ISBN 0-933849-59-1 Full Color

by Lindsay Wolter, age 9
Cheshire, Connecticut
ISBN 0-933849-61-3 Full Color

by Anna Riphahn, age 13
Topeka, Kansas
ISBN 0-933849-62-1 Full Color

by Micha Estlack, age 17
Yukon, Oklahoma
ISBN 0-933849-63-X Full Color

by Alexandra Whitney, age 8
Eugene, Oregon
ISBN 0-933849-64-8 Full Color

by Gillian McHale, age 10
Doylestown, Pennsylvania
ISBN 0-933849-65-6 Full Color

The Incredible Jelly Bean Day
Written and Illustrated by Taylor Maw

by Taylor Maw, age 17
Visalia, California
ISBN 0-933849-66-4 Full Color

Books Created By Students For Students Are Amazing

That's true! BOOKS FOR STUDENT BY STUDENTS® are absolutely amazing. They dazz They astound. They inform. And they delight.

All the stories are beautifully, thoughtfully, and cleverly written. And the illustratio are outstanding displays of artistic talents and skills.

Some of the books are so funny, they will make you laugh aloud. And some of t books are so touching, they will bring tears to your eyes.

The books do all the things that really good books do because they really are go books. When you see these exceptional books, you are bound to be proud of the st dents who created them. And you will be thrilled to share them with your students.

These are important books, too. Not only do they inform and entertain, but they also ha the power to motivate and inspire your students to write and illustrate their own books.

Written & Illustrated by...
a revolutionary two-brain approach for teaching students how to write and illustrate amazing books

David Melton

96 Pages • Illustrated • Softcover
ISBN 0-933849-00-1

Written & Illustrated by... by David Meltor

This highly acclaimed teacher's manual offers classroom-proven, step-by-ste instructions in all aspects of teaching students how to write, illustrate, assembl and bind original books. Loaded with information and positive approaches th really work. Contains lesson plans, more than 200 illustrations, and suggested ada tations for use at all grade levels – K through college.

The results are dazzling!
– Children's Book Review Service, Inc.

...an exceptional book! Just browsing through it stimulates excitement for writing.
– Joyce E. Juntune, Executive Director
American Creativity Association

A "how-to" book that really works!
– Judy O'Brien, Teach

WRITTEN & ILLUSTRATED BY... provides current of enthusiasm, positive thinki and faith in the creative spirit of childrer David Melton has the heart of a teacher.
– THE READING TEACH

Steven Shepard
age 13

Karen Kerber
age 12

Kristin Pedersen
age 18

Lisa Butenhoff
age 13

Heidi Salter
age 19

Lisa Gross
age 12

Duba Kolanović
age 18

Amy Jones
age 17

Adam Moore
age 9

Cara Reichel
age 15